Fall of a Demigod
(Tales of Odealeous)

A.J. Martinez

A.J Martinez

Fall Of A Demi God

In the sky over the Kumo Sora Mountains of the Yama country, lived the Effeelions. Mystical creatures that lived away from society. Their city floated in the sky like a swan on a river. Mythologists have said that the Effeelions evolved from Elves and that their magic is greater than those of legend. Peaceful creatures of meditation, knowledge seekers, nomadic and could live for hundreds of years. However, not many had seen an Effeelion. They never left their home in the sky and when they did, they used their magic and disguised themselves as birds and other feather creatures. They were ghost to the world and they wished to never be seen by anyone. Many have tried to search for their city in the sky but have failed countless times. No one had ever flown high enough or searched the sky long enough to find the mystical city.

The Effeelions only trusted one person. That one person lived among them. A demigod who had been touched by a star of the night and gifted with cosmic power. A demigod who had been blessed by Aeramus, the dragon god of air. The demigod lived in an island that floated next to the grand city of the Effeelions. For fifty years he had lived with the

5

lovable creatures. Fifty years as a demigod. Fifty years since he surrendered the mortal life. The night was his and the stars were his. At the very flick of his fingers he could make the stars move and summon a meteor shower down to Odealeous. He could fly riding the winds with no wings on his back.

Caim was his name or at least that is the name the Effeelions gave him when Aeramus blessed him and made him immortal. He was the guardian of Kazenolumos, the sky city. He was also part of the Effeelion's research team called Feathered Ghost. They traveled the world in search of answers that would lead them to the higher spiritual being called Cosmus that they sought for so long.

One day, Caim woke with only one thought in mind. He planned to leave Kazenolumos for a day and swoop down to the Yama country. In his hut on the floating island, he stared out the window at the romantic view of the sun. He ate toricarrots, a vegetable that grew in the farms that floated east of the sky city. As he bit on the burly raw vegetable, he thought of her. The human girl of the Yama country. He was eager to see her again after busy months traveling Odealeous with the Feathered Ghost.

He walked outside of his hut almost naked with only underwear covering his privates. He inhaled and wind swirled around his body. Feathers danced around and the wind seemed to bind him. He then exhaled and as he released his breath, he became clothed in green, white and yellow colors. He wore a long green tunic embroidered with golden feathers and a white turtleneck underneath. As the winds blew, they filled his large sleeves with air. His pants were green and white. Gravel crunched below his strap sandals. He stretched and yawned loudly, lazily.

"Hopefully the elders won't have any task for me today. Here I come, Kairi," he said as he munched on the toricarrot. He took one final bite and then tossed the remaining aside.

"You should know better than to litter, Caim," said a voice from his right.

"I am fertilizing. I was hoping some toricarrot crops begin to grow by my hut's front yard." Caim responded without looking at the person.

"You think you are so clever," said an Effeelion approaching from a tree nearby. She stood four feet tall with white hair wearing a yellow tunic with large sleeves.

Caim looked down at the short Effeelion almost half his size. Her pointy ears were long passed her head. A small nose and eyes big and glary like those of a kitten. "Lanalynn my dear friend. Today I am off duty. Please come back tomorrow. If there are any tasks for me then leave a note on my door and hope the wind does not blow it away."

"Your sense of humor is annoying, Caim," Lanalynn said.

"The morning is still young, Lanalynn. Swiftly tell me why you're visiting. I have things I like to do today," Caim said as he yawned, digging his knuckles in his eyes.

"Elder Nehushine wishes to speak to you," Lanalynn said.

"Oh I see. A lecture. In that case please do leave a note on my door. Thank you and have a good day." With those last words Caim levitated off the grass as if gravity had no effect on him. He began to fly away from his hut and left the floating island.

"Caim listen to me!" Lanalynn yelled before Caim flew any farther. He was just dozens of feet away from her and over the trees that circled around his hut.

"Hurry it up now," Caim said impatiently.

"What if I told you that you are in trouble with the council of seven." Lanalynn hoped to catch Caim's attention a bit longer. The demigod had a short attention span and lost interest rather quickly.

"Don't be silly. If I had done anything that would upset the council than Nehushine would be the one knocking on my door," Caim replied and quickly flew away from the island.

He flew high in the open sky. Clouds below formed a field of white like snow and through the openings in the clouds, Caim could see the Yama country. To his right floated Kazenolumos. It was made of marvel as well as other rare stones, gold and a white heavenly steel the Effeelions called zeustoss. It was built in three sections in the shape of a pyramid. Inside each section lived thousands of Effeelions and at the very top resided the leaders of the race called the council of seven whom Caim worked with. It was never a boring sight and the city walls were bedecked with gold, gleaming in the sunlight.

Caim loved it so much. As much as he loved flying. He then took his mind off the city and onto the Yama country below. He dived like an eagle falling on its prey. Head down and the wind whistling over his ears. He closed his eyes until he was below the clouds and on the vast skies of Odealeous. The country looked small from up high, like looking at a map on a turquoise table.

His palms were wide open by his hips and unleashed a blast of air that applied more force on his fall. He spun playfully as he fell from the sky, like a child dizzying himself. As he got closer he began to see the Kumo Sora Mountains of the Yama country. The person who waited for him lived in a valley near those mountains. The mountains were named after the Effeelions, although no human other than Caim saw the evolved Elves. It's been fifty years since he called himself a human. A part of him missed the mortal life for personal reasons, however his mind was set. Today he flew down to have a little "fun."

He began to ease his fall once he was at the level of the mountains. To the east was the Yumeh River and south of the Kumo Sora Mountains was Yumemaru Town, where he would meet her. The town was built in a valley. Green hills sloped on the town. As he began to fly over the city, he shifted into a hawk. His body shrank into a feathered creature. He shrieked as a bird and descended. Once he saw the border, he dived down into an alley where no one could see him shift and stood as a human again. He did not want any attention from the town's people.

He walked through the alley, stone walls to his left and right. He turned right at an intersection and then sprinted down the cobbled street. The people were energetic and the town was always busy. It was not the first time Caim had visited Yumemaru town. He had been visiting this one person for six months. *It is not much but as a demigod, perhaps I can make up for the time I lost*, he thought as he ran pass a group of people wearing pointy hats, hauling water on their shoulders. Soon he reached the border of the town where she waited by a gate.

There she stood. She was beautiful. Narrow dark eyes and her hair was raven black. Her skin was pale like vanilla. She wore what the people of the Yama country called a Kimono. It was green with flower illustrations swirling up. Her sleeves were large much like the ones of Caim's tunic. Her long hair cascaded on her back and shoulders. She smiled when she saw him running towards her.

"Did you miss me?" he asked, staring into her narrow lovely dark eyes.

"How could I not? I dreamt of your white hair," she told him. Caim blushed and stroked his white hair.

His hair was similar to the Effeelions. It was part of his gift from Aeramus. He embraced her and she pressed her face into his chest. They kissed deeply and long to savor all the days that they had been away from each other. It seemed like months had passed since they last held each other closely but it had only been seven days.

They held hands and walked away from the town and onto the fields of rice. They walked on a path between the crops of rice. Caim could not take his eyes off her. She was beautiful but that is not why he fell for her. He had seen many beautiful things in his travels throughout the world but she was like a rare glowing jewel he found at the bottom of a river. Kairi was her name. A name he thought about every day.

His only fear was that his Effeelion friends and the council in Kazenolumos would find out about her.

"What is it?" she asked. Her voice so gentle it could melt butter.

"Nothing, just thinking about this place," he answered.

"You've lived here before?" she asked. He looked up at the sky remembering the days of his youth when he once lived in Yumemaru town as a human.

"Yes," he answered. "Once, when I was young. I lived here alone for many years. Then I left to become a monk in the mountains."

"Why you never told me that. How long ago was this?" she asked him and he looked away again.

He was afraid she would see the lies in his eyes. How could she see such things? *I am a demigod*, he told himself. *She cannot see into my soul unless I allow her.* He was aware of his abilities as a demigod. He was only half or a small fraction of what an ideal god would be like. He was immortal and could not die as simple as a human would.

"It was only about five years ago. I don't remember everything," he answered and held her hand. She gently pulled his hand away and stopped on the path. She grabbed his face and stared into his lavender eyes.

"You told me that you were from the east of Yama. Are you lying to me?"

"No! Good dragon gods. I am not lying," he said. If he was still human he would be nervous by now. "I lived in Yumemaru town for five years then I became a monk in the mountains. However, before all of that, I was living in a village, east of the capital."

"I don't like liars," Kairi said and Caim turned his cheek. "Look at me." Kairi grabbed his face and gently turned it. "Why are you lying to me?" she asked suspiciously.

"I am not lying. It's just complicated," Caim answered. "Why does that matter so much?"

"It has been six months and I have enjoy being with you," she said and caressed his cheek. "Yet I feel as though there is something I am not seeing clearly."

"With time you will know. I promise. It is not easy to explain." Caim frowned. They touched foreheads with closed eyes and kissed.

"I have never asked you this but where are your mother and father?" Kairi asked again eagerly. She had never seen Caim accompanied by anyone. It was usually the two of them and then they would part ways at dusk.

"I never knew my parents," Caim answered. He could

not stare at her after that question. It brought lonely memories.

"I am sorry. I didn't mean to…" Kairi could not finish her sentence.

"Do not worry," Caim said and kissed her again.

They continued walking through the field of rice on a dirt path. They walked far away from Yumemaru town. Caim took Kairi to a river after the farmlands. Tall oak trees and bushes cast large shadows over them, hoping that no one from the village would spot them. They jumped in the water, nude, and swam in the warm river. They dived deep and hugged and watched fishes of all sorts of colors swimming by. Their bodies pressed and Caim entered her and kissed her. She dug her nails in his back and bit him. They went up to the surface and Caim took her on top of a large smooth rock. When they were done, they sat by the river bank. There was no one around in the area of the river so for the moment it was safe there.

They got dressed and rested under a cherry blossom tree. The pink leaves fell on them as they conversed about the first time they meet.

"Why is your hair white?" Kairi asked, resting her head on his chest.

"I had told you before. I was born like this," he answered. "My hair has always been white. I have always been different."

"The first time we meet I thought you were old. It was funny. I used to make fun of you." Kairi caressed his face. Gently rubbing and kissing him. *I am not sure how long this will last but I will cherish every moment. Oh Kairi why couldn't I find you before,* Caim could only ponder. She was eighteen years old and daughter of a wealthy man in Yumemaru town. Although he was a demigod, he still had humanly desires. He longed for such intimacy in his human life and now was to be the perfect time after so many decades. Still, he was not sure how to tell her of who he really was. He could not simply break the oath he had with the Effeelions and start a life with Kairi as he so fantasized.

"Caim, why did you stop being a monk?" Kairi asked, innocently.

Such questions of his old days bothered him but he could not ignore her. He only hoped that one day he won't have to cut off his tongue.

"One day they told me that I did not meet their criteria. Monks are very detached from earthy things and one day I did something that was unacceptable for them," Caim explained.

"What did you do?" Kairi asked.

"I fell in love. Monks are not allowed to fall in love.

Their only love is the spiritual life and their dedication to the gods and goddesses."

Kairi's eyes softened. They kissed again and continued talking about each other's life until dusk came. It was time for Kairi to leave.

"I told my mother that I would be with my friends by the river. I promised to be home by dusk," she explained.

"Understood," Caim replied.

This was how it usually was whenever he came to see her. Time stood still whenever they were together but when twilight came and the sun painted the sky with red and orange, the clock ticked again and they went their separate ways.

Caim stood up; ready to walk Kairi back to town but then he saw a figure hovering over the river. If he was a human he would have been greatly frightened and disturbed. Kairi shrieked and hid behind Caim. She shuddered and stepped farther away from the river. Caim stood his ground and stared at the figure that hovered over the river. It had a white mask with a triangle opening for the left eye and an "X" slashed on the area of the mouth. He saw the eye blink inside the mask and realized that it was a human. Whoever it was, they were clad in black. His or her cloak ruffled in the wind. It was like looking at a crow standing on a tree branch. It made one feel dead as if one's life was withering.

"Who are you?" Caim shouted at the stranger in black.

The stranger in black did not reply. The stranger flew away. It was odd for Caim. The stranger flew effortless with no wings. Caim sensed no maju from the stranger so he was not sure if they were using aeromancy. He was the only one that he knew that could fly in such a way. Only him and the Effeelions. Even with maju, the source of energy within a person, most mages would not be able to fly so easily.

"What was that?" Kairi asked with a shaky frightened voice.

"I don't know but it looks like it has no interest in us," Caim said and placed his hand over her waist. "Come on. Let's take you home." Caim walked with her, making sure that she arrived home before nightfall.

They parted ways by the entrance of Yumemaru town. Caim watched her walk away. There was something about her departure that he enjoyed. It was not her beauty that put him at ease. Her narrow dark eyes, smooth pale skin like vanilla and long raven black hair. It was not her beauty. It was the bliss she helped him gain. The warmth he felt in his chest holding her hand. The tenderness of their togetherness. The love he never experienced before he became a demigod kissed by the stars and blessed by Aeramus. The day felt long with her by his side and the stars were beginning to shine in the night. *It was a fun day reliving my human life*, Caim said to himself. Relishing all the things that his powers helped him acquire.

Caim ran to the field of rice. He ran far away from Yumemaru town and surveyed the area making sure no one was around to see him jet off the ground. His vast maju carried him high up in the sky, rapidly. He flew until he was as high as the mountains. Caim paused and spun to take one last look at the town below. Lantern lights illuminated the streets. He pictured himself with her one last time. He had promised her that he would return to Yumemaru town within seven days.

The wind swirled around him and he blasted up towards Kazenolumos. Through a large opening in the clouds he saw the stars shining. He ascended and spun creating a twister of clouds. Beyond the sky, the stars danced as Caim spun. They moved and shined in a circular motion like a glittering whirlpool. It was his cosmic power causing the stars to sway. He was in such a blissful mood that he could call upon a comet if he desired. He swooped in and out of the clouds, diving through the wetness and rested on them like a field of sheep wool. He watched the stars dancing above and they formed a constellation for Kairi in her Kimono. *If only it could last forever,* he thought dreamingly. *But she is mortal like I once was. Maybe I can convert her.* He fantasized about the possibilities. He had the power. He knew he could. *I think I can turn her into a demigod like me.*

He snapped out of his day dream and blasted towards Kazenolumos. The city's gold shone with moonlight. The city had a barrier. It was like a bubble and it protected the sanctuary. No one could see its transparent barrier except in the sunlight. Caim flew gently through, making sure it did not trigger any alarms. It only worked on unknown folks who might threaten the city. No one but the Effeelions and Caim were allowed.

Caim flew towards the island east of the floating city. He descended down and gusted the trees. Down below he saw them. Three members of the council of seven and Lanalynn stood outside his hut. *What in Odealeous could they want at this time of day?* he thought, unpleasantly. When his feet touched the ground, he paced towards them.

Nehushine stroked his triangular long beard that cascaded from his chin. He was the head of the council of seven. He was five hundred and ten years old. The three members of the council wore turtleneck robes with swirling illustrations on them.

Nehushine was clad in orange and the two females Areira and Kazemee wore green and blue.

"Had a splendid day I see," Nehushine commented.

"Indeed," Caim replied and crossed his arms with a smile. "I hope you are not here to ruin it my good lord."

"Now why would I want to do that? Unless the guardian of Kazenolumos was up to no good of course," Nehushine said. His eyes were icy and thin. He stared at Caim suspiciously.

"Dear council. You block the path to my hut. So… do you have a surprise for me?" Caim asked, sarcastically. "If not, then I invite you inside for a cup of tea… Actually on second thought, I am rather tire. I think I will go to sleep."

"Sorry to burst your air bubble, Caim," Areira said from Nehushine's left. She had brown hair; her face was sharp with small lips. "We know about you and that human girl."

If Caim was a mortal man as he was five decades ago, then he would be sweating. His heart would have been hammering his chest. At that moment he felt none of those things but he could not lie to the council. "This is a really sensitive topic. How about if we discuss this tomorrow? I am tire and would like to go to sleep please." Caim had a lot of freedom in

Kazenolumos. He tried to dodge the conversation and wanted to hide in his hut or runaway.

"You think of yourself so highly that you believe we are easily fooled?" Kazemee asked. She was clad in blue and had tan skin and her eyes shined a gold yellow. Caim always found her annoying.

"Technically, yes I do. We do live in the clouds after all. We are like gods for the humans below. Need I remind you?" the demigod replied.

"Caim. Demigods don't feel tire. Your body does not need rest unless you actually want to." Kazemee gave Caim no place to hide. She always broke his verbal defenses and his jokes fogged right through her.

Blast her, Caim thought. *Of course demigods don't feel tire. What a stupid excuse.*

"Lord Nehushine, you have never told me why this chestnut is part of the council." Caim mocked the tan Effeelion. She snarled at him like a cat but it only made Caim laugh.

"That is not for you to judge, demigod," Nehushine said. "Meet us at the third level tower and we shall speak about you and this human girl you have been mingling with. This is an order. You will be scanned by the council of seven. This is a very serious case. "

Caim felt foolish. He thought he was hiding it rather

well. Unless someone had spied on him while he was away. Who could have known where he was or what he was doing? Caim looked at his friend Lanalynn who hid behind the three council members. Caim stared at her as she peeked from behind Lady Kazemee.

"Lanalynn were you spying on me?" he asked.

The Effeelion frowned and stared at the ground, ashamed for being a tattle tale.

"I was worried and didn't know what to do? So I spoke to the council about it first," Lanalynn confessed. "Forgive me, Caim, but you know we are not supposed to affiliate with humans in such a way. Why did you fall in love with that human?"

"My dear Lanalynn," Nehushine interrupted. "Do not apologize. You were right to report Caim. We are all concern. As much as I dislike getting into your personal business, Caim, this is something that can affect us all. Meet us at the third level tower, immediately." Nehushine demanded, not forcefully but with duty, as a father would.

The Effeelions were gentle people. They disliked confrontations. However, when such serious matters occurred they always tried to solve the problem immediately. Their priority was peace and love in their sanctuary.

The three council members and Lanalynn walked away. Kazemee stuck her tongue out at Caim. He winced. The four Effeelions took flight. Their air magic levitated them off the ground and they flew towards the city. Caim sighed and kicked the dirt. *I can't blame Lanalynn for this,* he thought. *This is my fault and yet I devoted my life for the Effeelions. For the air dragon god. I assist the Feathered Ghosts in hunting down information throughout the world. I thought a little happiness would not hurt anyone. I know the law of this kingdom. I know my duty. I only ask for a little mortal bliss.*

Caim was willing to take full responsibility for his actions. However, he was not willing to let go of Kairi.

He kicked off the ground and blasted towards the third level tower of Kazenolumos. He ascended higher in the vast sky of the night. He looked at the colossal columns that held the second level over the first level and third above. The wind whipped and lashed his body as he jetted towards the third level. A tower rose and at the very top of the tower was the dome of the council of seven. He entered through the window and with a loud thump he landed in a kneeling pose. Everyone in the room startled at his dynamic entrance.

"Must you always make such a flamboyant appearance?" Nehushine asked sitting in a hemispheric platform. Among him sat the council of

seven. They all sat crossed legged. To the right sat
Tortori an Effeelion with a big beard and bushy eye
brows. Then Tweng, a white hair Effeelion and next
to him sat Kazemee the tan female Effeelion that
Caim called a chestnut. In the center Nehushine sat
stroking his triangular long white beard that cascaded
from his chin. To Nehushine's left sat Areira then the
twins Nova Linda and Nova Luna. The twins dressed
similarly. Their clothes contained many feathers that
gave a peak shape to their shoulders and waist.

 They all stared at him solemnly for the demigod was
highly respected yet at times they would compare him
to a child. The Effeelions were no taller than four
feet. Caim was nearly six feet tall. They had long
pointy ears, small noses like cats and air magic that
could summon twisters throughout Odealeous. Caim
loved them. He listened to the council of seven and
learned the knowledge they had acquired throughout
centuries. Although his magic and powers were of a
demigod, his mind was very human like. He
understood the differences between himself and the
Effeelions. Hardly ever would there be any trouble,
quarrels or drama. However, this day was different.

Caim looked up and noticed the blurry moons in the
mosaic ceiling of the dome. Since the council now
knew of his secret, Caim knew that many things
would change for him.

"Demigod Caim." Nehushine began. "We have

summoned you here today because we disapprove of your activities down in the Yama country. You are endangering us by associating yourself with this human."

"Yes Lord Nehushine. Explain to me how I am bringing doom upon Kazenolumos," Caim debated. "What scrolls have you read that speak of demigods falling in love with humans and bringing doom to the people of the sky?"

"Settle down good god of the stars." Nehushine waved his hand gesturing Caim to lower his voice. The long bearded Effeelion then looked across the crescent platform at the twins, Nova Linda and Nova Luna. "Novas. Can you please read Caim's vow to the Effeelions and to the dragon god of air."

The twins lifted a scrolled that lied between them. They opened it up together horizontally each holding a side of the scroll. The paper was brown and the pommel of the scroll was golden. Caim remembered that scroll yet he showed no expression towards it. The twins read the scroll together.

I Caim blessed with air magic by Aeramus himself swear to protect the city of Kazenolumos. I will wed no woman of Odealeous or have offsprings. I vow to be on the path to enter the realm of Cosmus with the Effeelions. The realm of the highest enlightened beings. I vow to hunt for information throughout Odealeous with the Feathered Ghosts team. My duty is to the people of Kazenolumos and the goal of the Effeelions. Our purpose is to one day enter the realm of Cosmus and discover true and everlasting enlightenment. We are ghost to humanity. We are high beings who evolved from Elves and the Elves that evolved from humans. I make this vow and swear to Aeramus to do my duties.

Demigod Caim.

The twins then rolled back the scroll. Nehushine continued to stroke his beard staring at Caim. The demigod scratched his head and dug his pinky finger in his ear as if he wasn't listening. Nehushine nodded his head disappointed. "Why oh why were you chosen by the air dragon god?" Nehushine asked the divine.

"When you have an answer to that question please knock on my door and let me know," Caim remarked.

"What do you have to say about your vow to the Effeelions?" Tortori asked who was a friend of Caim.

"Are you hoping I say something idiotic Lord Tortori?" Caim said with a cocky tone.

"Watch how you speak to the council young man?" Tortori told Caim. His lips hid under his bushy white beard.

"I am not a young man. I am seventy years old. My powers keep me young but I have been living here since I was twenty years of age." Caim debated.

"Perhaps you still see me as a child but don't forget who stopped the war between the Yama country and United Pathways. The two countries would have destroyed each other had I not stopped them. As for the vows I made to the Effeelions. I know what I am doing. I do my duty like any other Effeelion in this city. Perhaps you should read the scroll again my good lords and ladies of the council but there is nothing there that says that a demigod cannot affiliate himself with a human."

"Caim we are ghost to humanity. The Effeelions cannot allow themselves to be seen by a human," Nehushine argued.

"Take a good look at me Lord Nehushine. I am not an Effeelion," Caim answered. It hurt him to make such a remark. He did not want to differentiate himself from the people of Kazenolumos but he disliked denying himself of the truth. The council of seven gasped. They flabbergasted at the demigod's words.

"By the howling winds. Caim, you are one of us. Not by blood or flesh and bones but we consider you to be family," said Lady Areira. "There are tons of Effeelion girls that would love to mate with such a mighty young man."

"Please stop calling me a young man. What I would like to know is why the council of seven dislikes the idea of me coming in contact with a human." It was such an uncomfortable thing to talk about for Caim. He felt naked before the council of seven. He expected a better understanding from them since they were all hundreds of years of age.

"Allow me to explain demigod of the wind and stars," Tweng said who sat next to Kazemee. "You might lose the powers that Aeramus granted you the day after you stopped the war between the two countries. You are a high being just like us regardless of the roots of your race. We see that you still have fleshy human desires and…"

"Stop right there Lord Tweng." Caim halted the councilor's speech. "Please do explain how my fleshy desires will cause me to lose my powers?"

"Well not only will you be breaking the rules and your vows," Tweng continued. "But getting emotionally closer to that human girl will bring you down to earth. Meaning that you will be too attached to her to pursue the path you have chosen towards Cosmus. Your vow says you will not wed any women of Odealeous or have offsprings of human blood. Your relationship with this human girl will cause you to lose your powers. Both the gift of Aeramus and perhaps your cosmic powers."

Caim remained silent after Lord Tweng had spoken. He was right. Caim was breaking his vows. Although he sought fleshy desires, he had become oblivious to know that he could not have such relationships with a human girl. He eyeballed the council again and said, "The human girl Kairi does not bear my child."

"And you know this how?" Nehushine asked leaning forward, still stroking his white beard. If Caim was mortal at that very moment he would be nervous. He was unsure if Kairi was pregnant. He had been seeing her for six months but her belly had not swell with his child yet. They had made love countless times. Suddenly he became aware of the possibility. *Good dragon gods, what now?* he thought.

"Your silence speaks for itself Caim," Neshushine said solemnly. "We love you my dear boy. You have been living with us since the age of twenty however, we see you as a son. We are concern about you. If you lose your powers we lose a guardian. Ever since you joined us Caim we have made incredible discoveries. We believe that we are getting closer to finding a way into the realm of Cosmus. Your cosmic powers have done incredible things for the Effeelions. I will confess that for the past five decades you have been a great asset to our court and to our people. We ask that you continue your path seeking the realm of Cosmus. We do not wish to ruin your happiness but we advice that you think about the decisions you are making."

Caim loved the Effeelions. How could he lose sight

of the very promise he made. He would leave it all behind for what. For fleshy bliss. For a love that he only knew for six months compared to five decades. He then thought of the days when he first received his powers. The day when he saw that shooting star and absorbed its power using the cosmo lantern. The magic tool that he found in the mountains when he was a monk. When he absorbed the shooting star and gained cosmic powers, his life changed. When the Yama country was at war with the United Pathways, he was able to stop both armies. Then the Effeelions revealed themselves before him. They asked for his help and Caim accepted gracefully. Aeramus the dragon god of air whom had helped the Effeelions evolve, gifted Caim with extraordinary air magic. Caim wanted to change the world and do great things. The Effeelions had shown him a path that he pursued with love.

However, for the past few years a different desire had been lurking inside the demigod. He wanted to relive his human life once more but he did not want to take his eyes off his goal. He wanted to grasp both but he feared he would have to let go of one.

"If this human girl gives birth to your half breed, will you allow her to raise your child, Caim?" Kazemee asked him as he mulled about his past.

"If she gives birth to my child then I will take full responsibility," Caim said. "He will be a demigod just like his father. I will raise him myself here in Kazenolumos."

"And what will you do about this human girl?" Nehushine asked.

"I am sorry for coming in contact with Kairi. I will tell her that I cannot see her again," Caim answered.

"Very well then I believe we have a good understanding here," Nehushine concluded. "This case is close. Caim, you may leave."

Caim turned to the window without hesitation. He did not have any last words for the council of seven but before he left…

"Caim wait!" Areira called to him.

The demigod spun around and met eyes with Lady Areira.

"Yes my lady."

"This is for the best," she said softly.

Caim gave her a long smirk and chuckled. He then turned back to the window above and blasted out into the night sky.

Part 2

The next day, Caim pondered in his hut of the eastern floating islands. The sun glared through his window and blinded his lavender eyes. He sipped green tea while contemplating the romantic view of the morning sun. He could not sleep. Although he did not need sleep, he would usually rest for at least five hours. He could not stop thinking of Kairi and wondered if she bear his child. He would be a father soon and did not spoke to his Effeelion friends about it. *They would not understand such humanly issues*. He wrote his thoughts in his journal. Caim enjoyed writing. His private world was in there. From things he experienced as a demigod to personal things he dared not whisper. He wrote stories to pass the time when he was not working with the Effeelions or on some trip throughout Odealeous.

He wrote about how eager he was to one day find the realm of Cosmus where the Effeelions believed Caim gained his cosmic powers. Caim wrote about his humanly desires and how he never lived the life of a regular human boy. His parents had died on a ship traveling from a northern country to the Yama country. He still remembered very clearly how the ocean waves reigned over and sunk the ship. He wrote about how he was very lonely in the Yama country. *Even as a demigod I guess one cannot have it all.*

While alone with his thoughts in his hut, writing and drinking tea, someone knocked on the door. He stood up; his knee hit the table and knocked over the elegant cup of tea. The green tea spilled over his journal and blurred his words. Caim was annoyed. "That is not a good sign," he said, hoping he was wrong.

He answered the door and saw Lanalynn sweating and panting. "We are in trouble" she said, her voice shaky and low as if to cry.

"What do you mean?" Caim asked calmly. Lanalynn ran and wrapped her arms around his waist. She pressed her head against his belly and shivered.

"Lanalynn, my dear. What is happening?" Caim asked in deep concern.

"Someone is attacking the town. Clad in black with a white mask. Caim, everyone is trying to stop him but he is too strong," Lanalynn said as she sobbed.

Caim knelt to be at the same head height as Lanalynn. He grabbed her gently and looked into her big kitten eyes.

"Has the council of seven been notified of this?" Caim asked.

"They are fighting the intruder with everything they've got. Many of my friends have died already. Please Caim, do something." Lanalynn begged. Her eyes damped.

For a moment Caim felt nervous. A feeling he had not felt in decades. But only a wisp of nervousness. Such a small stroke of fear like a mosquito bite. Caim kissed Lanalynn on the forehead and said, "Stay away from danger. Find your family and flee the city until I get rid of this intruder."

Caim ran out of his house and kicked off the ground faster than he ever had before. Wind whistling and lashing around his body, he rushed towards Kazenolumos. *An intruder in Kazenolumos*, he thought as he flew. *That is impossible. It has been five decades of guarding this sanctuary. No one has ever found this city. An omen in deed.*

In the second level of the sky city, Caim caught a glimpse of the Effeelions fighting the foe. Caim could hear the people screaming. He pressed more maju into his flight and blasted through the sky and into the city. He saw dozens of Effeelions lying on the marvel floors. Some bleeding and injured and some had fainted on the floor. Caim landed dynamically and quickly surveyed the area. He followed the screams and dashed, his feet gliding over the stone floors. Some houses were destroyed and pillars toppled. Mothers carrying children ran. Brothers and sisters of long pointy ears, four feet tall, fled holding hands, never leaving their love ones behind.

Down the ivory street he felt the winds gusting. He sensed the Effeelions maju casting air spells. He felt one large maju fading away. *It must be one of the councils*, Caim assumed. He dashed down the streets and there he saw him. The intruder clad in black. He wore a white mask with a triangle opening for the left eye and an "X" slashed on the area for the mouth. *I have seen him before*, Caim remembered. *Yes I know him but…*

Caim could not help but think that he was guilty for the suffering of the Effeelions today. It was the same masked stranger that saw him and Kairi by the river in the Yama country. Had he followed Caim here? So high in the clouds…. Impossible.

The intruder in black used air magic sending three Effeelions flying towards Caim. The demigod caught the three Effeelions in the air with open arms and set them on the ground. "Get out of here," he barked at them. They nodded and flew away from danger.

Caim noticed that five elders of the council of seven surrounded the intruder in black. Nehushine, Kazemee, Tweng, Tortori and Areira. The twins were missing.

Tweng and Tortori molded their maju and cast sharp winds upon the intruder. The wind whipped and rushed from the two elders and aimed to cleave the intruder vertically. The intruder gave a loud roar and reversed their spells with his own maju. Tweng and Tortori dodged their own spells. The sharp winds destroyed columns around the city and down the ivory street.

"Council of seven, hear me!" Caim shouted. "Leave this fight to me. Help the people instead. I will rid us of this intruder."

"Perhaps you will give me a better fight than these pointy ear midgets," said the intruder. His voice echoed inside his mask. "Caim is you name. Am I right? Just the demigod I have been hunting for."

"What motive do you have for attacking this sanctuary and how in Odealeous did you find us?" Caim leered the intruder in black.

"First of all, allow me to introduce myself. My name is Jairo." The intruder bowed spreading his long black cloak as if it were a gown and feminine. "It was not so difficult to find this lovely city. All I did was follow a little love bird to his cage. I am sure you remember me."

Caim had seen this stranger before. He began to feel the guilt. He led this stranger into the city. This intruder had followed Caim somehow. It made no sense. *I would have sensed his maju if he had been following me*, Caim thought. *I can't sense any maju from this stranger. It's as if he was a corpse.*

"Yes little birdie. I saw you with your little girlfriend by the river. I knew who you were. Your cosmic powers were like a magnet to me. I could not resist it. I had to hunt you down and look where you lead me to. The legendary city of the Effeelions." Jairo laughed. He levitated off the ground. Caim was not sure if it was air magic but he could not sense any maju coming from this man.

"Caim be careful," Nehushine said. His forehead was bleeding and he stood over the debris of a stone house. "His powers are similar to yours."

"That is impossible, Lord Nehushine. I am the only individual I know that has cosmic powers," Caim said and stared at the white masked stranger.

"Listen to the geezer," Jairo mocked. "He knows who he is up against."

Caim stepped closer to Jairo fearlessly till he was only six feet away from the foe. He faced Jairo and looked into the triangle opening for the left eye. "Unless you want to die I command that you leave this fortress right now." Caim threatened but such simple words had no effect on Jairo.

"You are allowing me to flee after I made such a mess in your city," Jairo paraphrase with a cocky tone and giggled. "How generous and stupid of you. I expected to hear more vigorous words from the guardian of Kazenolumos. I came all this way to see this dull figure of a demigod. White hair like an old hag and with humanly dreams of a child." Jairo laughed hysterically. Caim could only stare at Jairo with disgust. He felt no anger only annoyance. The council of seven fled the area, leaving Caim alone with the masked intruder. Caim wanted to punish this foe for ruining the beautiful city that the Effeelion spent millenniums to build. White Marble pillars and homes made of stone. The houses that piled over each other and gave shape to the inner city had fallen throughout the second level. Caim gazed up at the high ceiling of the second level. The golden paint that illustrated owls, hawks, sparrows and stars glittering. This sanctuary he so loved was to be destroyed by this one man who would not show his face.

"You laugh at me, destroy my city and murder my people. This will not go unpunished," Caim said, voice hoarse, seething with anger. He balled his hands into a fist and rubble began to elevate off the ground.

"Oh good. You are angry now. This will make things so much more fun. I was beginning to think you were but a mirthless hermit in the sky. Come now. Show me your godly powers." Jairo taunted and took an open legs and arms stance as if to grab the horns of a bull.

"Before I punish you, I want to know. Why did you do it?" Caim asked.

"To get your attention of course," Jairo replied. "Also, turning great cities into ruins is a hobby of mine. That is not the only reason why I am here. I came here for the Aero Cosmo Jewel. Of course, you know all about it already."

Caim felt as though this man had been stalking him for ages. "How do you know about the Aero Cosmo Jewel? The jewel is but a myth to the world."

"It might be a myth or a bedtime story to the world. However, for a treasure hunter like me, I always believed it was real. Thanks to you, my dreams are coming true. All the stories I read about the aero jewel were true. So if you love this floating rock of a city you better hand over the jewel, oh wise demigod." Jairo threw his long wide cloak over his body. Wind began to rush around him.

"The jewel will never be yours. The only way to get it is to kill me and in case you did not know, demigods don't die," Caim smirked. A cocky smirk of victory and justice. He knew that he was indestructible. He could not die. Not by a sword or a spell of any attribute.

"I refuse to believe that," Jairo responded. "Absolutely everything in Odealeous has a weakness.

Even the great dragon gods themselves have a weakness. I won't need to kill you to get what I want. In fact you are going to hand it over to me."

Hearing Jairo's last words enraged Caim. He extended his arms with palms wide open. Behind Jairo something oval appeared. It was like a hole that floated in thin air. Inside it, clouds moved and billowed. It was like staring through a window at the blue sky in daylight. Jairo was being sucked into the hole like a vacuum. The hole inhaled air like the nostrils of the mighty air dragon god himself. Jairo rebelled against the wind current.

"Very impressive. Oh mighty demigod," he said as the hole sucked him in. Jairo's long black cloak was caught by the hole. The hole vacuumed him in violently and Jairo used his maju to try and fly away from the air current. Caim hovered over debris with his arms crossed watching Jairo struggle.

"I hope your combat is better than your mouth," Caim said then he thrust his palm creating a pulse of air and pushed Jairo into the hole. Caim then flew into the hole following Jairo.

After they entered the portal, they were no longer in Kazenolumos. They were now leagues away from the sanctuary. They hovered in the sky staring each other down. The clouds below them were like a field of white sheep wool. The wind blew strong in such altitude.

"A portal?" Jairo questioned. "You can open portals. Absolutely amazing. This is cosmic magic you are using. I know it."

Caim made no remarks. He dashed through the air. Jairo prepared with wind dancing around his body. Caim opened another portal as he flew towards Jairo. The demigod flew into the portal. Jairo surveyed the skies. His opponent was nowhere in sight. The masked man only saw his own cloak billowing. Then Caim reappeared behind him. Jairo looked over his shoulder and just when he was about to twist his body and dodge, the demigod delivered a flying kick to his back. Pain blasted on Jairo's back and he heard his bones cracking. He felled down into the field of clouds.

Caim then opened another portal and made sure Jairo fell through it. Jairo reappeared above him and the demigod delivered a spinning kick to the side of his foe's head. Caim felt the solid material of the mask. It almost hurt him and he predicted it could be unbreakable.

Jairo fell through the clouds again. Two mighty kicks had been delivered. One on his back and one on the side of his face. Pain was blazing on those areas but he healed fast. He was prepared for such battle. He loved the pain. For Jairo it made the fight worthwhile and the more pleasurable it would be to destroy Kazenolumos and take the aero jewel with triumph.

Jairo used his maju to prevent himself from falling. He yelled and blasted through the sky towards the demigod. He saw the portal again. It was like a mirror reflecting the clouds. Jairo willingly flew into it as he molded maju. When his whole body had entered through the portal he saw Caim delivering another kick. At that very second Jairo unleashed a twister. The wind whistled like a million flutes playing a high pitch note. Caim was pushed away and Jairo remained in his position. The demigod was taken by the twister.

"A demigod should know better than to use the same trick so many times," Jairo criticized and swirled his hands controlling the twister. "You can't call yourself a god if you are so easily capture."

Caim's body was going with the current of the wild winds. As he orbited rapidly he almost felt helpless for a moment. *This is impossible*, he told himself. *I am Caim, demigod of the stars and wind. Blessed by Aeramus and baptized by the ocean of stars. I will not be defeated by this arrogant bastard.* Then he exploded with power. With a lion's roar he expanded his maju and broke the twister.

"Show me your cosmic power. Demigod!" Jairo demanded and laughed in high pitch.

"You want to see star power." Caim shouted. "I will show you the power of the stars. Powers from beyond the skies of Odealeous."

Spheres the size of marbles began to shine around Caim. They shined like the stars themselves. Dozens of them appeared. Then they began to multiply around Caim, shining red, blue, yellow and orange colors. Caim flew towards Jairo and the shining spheres followed him.

Jairo panicked and his heart pounded with excitement. *That is what I wanted to see.* From inside his cloak, black smoke billowed. Jairo summoned black birds much larger than ravens. The birds were ugly creatures with zombified eyes, bumpy beaks and boils on their heads. Their wings spread wide like that of an osprey. Hundreds of them flew from the black smoke.

"Do you think your birds can survive my star power?" Caim asked as his spheres danced around him. Small stars forged from his godly maju. No. He did not use maju to create these stars, he used pure cosmic energy but only a small amount. He still thought it was unnecessary to waste a large amount of power on this foe. His stars homed the ugly black birds that Jairo summoned. The birds swallowed the stars like they would swallow a fish and within seconds they blew up like fireworks.

The birds outnumbered Caim's stars. The demigod summoned more stars this time much bigger. He swung his arms and from every swing a star was hurled from the palm of his hands. The black birds swallowed his magic and exploded even greater. Soon all of Jairo's black birds died by Caim's power. After the birds were gone he surveyed the area. Jairo was not in sight.

"Perhaps he hides in the clouds," Caim assumed.

Abruptly, he felt something piercing his chest. He had not seen it. He had not felt the object move in his direction. The object plunged through his body. It was a sword of black steel. A steel that Caim detested. He groaned in pain but knew that he could not die. The sword could remain inside his body for years and the demigod could still live and breathe like a mortal. However, it made him weak and feverish. Caim looked over his shoulder and saw Jairo. Caim could not sense Jairo's maju. It was like trying to look for the soul of a dead man. Caim was always able to sense life. That is when he came to the conclusion that his foe was not human either.

"Kaminyte steel." Caim coughed and gripped the blade. "How did you know of my weakness?"

"I have studied all sorts of magic. I happen to know that cosmo is not the same as maju and only a few solid materials such as kaminyte steel can absorb such energy." Jairo chuckled behind Caim. The demigod chuckled as well and felt his cosmic power being drained.

"You are a fool. Even if you absorb my power you won't be able to defeat me. I am endless. I live forever. Your attempt is futile." Caim then grabbed the black steel, slid backwards on it and gripped Jairo's wrist.

Jairo lost grip of his sword and Caim twisted his wrist. The masked man kicked Caim in the face, gripped his sword and hovered backwards. His black blade dripped Caim's blood. The blood of a demigod. Jairo wiped it from his sword with his leather glove and it streamed down his forearm. He wanted to do something with that godly blood. He wanted to lick the blood off his own blade. It was sacred and carried cosmic energy. He knew of spells that he could cast with such blood.

"It is that cosmic power of yours that makes you a demigod," Jairo stated.

"Yes indeed. I am becoming impatient and I have come to the conclusion that you must not be kept alive. I will exterminate you from existence for attempting to destroy my city. Furthermore your lust for destruction will also harm many innocent humans in Odealeous. Such crime cannot be forgiven. I will now end your life." Caim increased his power. He swore to show no mercy. This time he would use a larger amount of power to destroy this villain and prevent him from spreading chaos. His body shined a lavender color and purple vapor rose from him.

"Ah yes. I can feel your cosmic powers increasing," Jairo said. "It is clear that I am no match for you. However, I did not come here today just to spar. I am here for the aero jewel and you are going to give it to me personally, Caim." Jairo spread his cloak wide open. Black smoke billowed like smoke stacks from a chimney. Heavy winds of the sky cleared the smoke revealing Jairo holding a young girl in a kimono. The girl's hair was long and black. Her skin pale. She panted in Jairo's arm and kicked in fear of falling. She shrieked and screamed. It was as if Jairo summoned her very being to his arms at will with his dark magic.

"Kairi," Caim gasped. As soon as he saw Kairi flailing in Jairo's arms, he decreased his power. He feared he might hurt her. He was in utter awe. Jairo's magic summoned the girl he loved with nothing but black smoke. *Dark magic*, the demigod assumed. *He had planned it. I am a fool. I should have stopped him the day I saw him hovering over the river in the Yama country.*

Jairo placed his sword over Kairi's neck. "Stop flailing, little girl. Unless you want to die."

"Don't you dare hurt her?" Caim yelled. He would not forgive himself if anything happened to his beloved. The mortal that he so loved. "Jairo, if you kill her. I am going to make sure you suffer a slow and extremely painful death. She is only human. She has nothing to do with the people of Kazenolumos."

The morning sun blazed above and the winds of the altitude blew softly now. Jairo laughed hysterically and gripped Kairi's neck. The girl began to cry. "Caim!" she yelled for her beloved. "Why am I here?" she cried and panted.

Caim felt guilt. Deep guilt. He now understood what the council of seven was trying to tell him. He then remembered the days of when he stopped the war between the Yama country and the United Pathways. The days when he first acquired his cosmic powers. The king of the Yama country asked Caim to help him win the war but Caim declined. He took no side and even tried to reason with the queen of the United Pathways. The advance country embarked to war to the shores of the Yama country. Caim used his powers to destroy their weapons and forced the boats to sail back to their lands. He was able to do it alone. He alone stopped a war but now he felt weak. He felt powerless to save the very girl he loved. A mortal of flesh and bones that could die any day unlike him.

"Why do you care so much?" Jairo said. He rubbed the black steel on Kairi's neck and the girl moaned with fear. "She can die at the thrust of my blade. You are willing to lower your powers for a mortal woman.

You are willing to give up your precious city of the sky for the pleasure of her wetness."

"Give me the girl, Jairo!" Caim yelled. He seethed with anger and his eyes began to glow white. "Don't you dare hurt her."

"Pathetic." Jairo spat. "A demigod with mortal desires. What a waste. It is true that beggars can't be choosers."

Caim froze. He was not sure what to do. He could open a portal and vacuum Jairo in it but then he would drive his blade inside Kairi. Caim thought of using razor winds to slice off Jairo's arms but he feared he might injure Kairi as well. He looked at the girl as she trembled in the hands of Jairo. Her dark eyes shed tears and she struggled to breath with Jairo's left hand on her windpipe.

"Tell me what you want Jairo. What will it take to prevent you from harming her?" Caim asked releasing his ego, submitting to the situation. *Oh mighty Aeramus dragon god of air, lend me your wit and wisdom to destroy this foe,* he prayed.

"I already told you what I want demigod," Jairo said. "How can you call yourself a demigod? It is obvious that I want to trade the girl for the aero jewel."

"You shall have the aero jewel." Caim surrendered. "Heed my words, Jairo. I will hunt you for this. May the dragon gods forgive you because I won't? Your actions today will boomerang upon you."

"Tender words," Jairo said sarcastically and snickered.

"Follow me." Caim beckoned.

The demigod led the way to the location of the aero jewel. He flew west from the morning sun. Jairo flew right behind him as he held Kairi with the black sword on her throat. The white masked man held her from her girth. Kairi held on to Jairo shrieking and crying. Caim looked back to make sure his beloved was fine. Just when he had promised the council of seven that he would not see her again, she returned to him in the form of danger. Would he still save her if he did not know her? His human self spoke louder than his godly side at that moment. Was he going to give Jairo the aero jewel in exchange for Kairi? Would he risk the Effeelion race for her? Was it worth it? He thought about it as he flew towards Kazenolumos. If he removed the aero jewel from its den then the entire city would fall from the sky.

The sky city was a speck on the horizon floating above the field of clouds. Caim had pushed the battle between him and Jairo leagues away from the city. *Please forgive me Nehushine and the council*, he prayed. *I promise I will find a way to save the city. Have faith in me Aeramus.* Once Caim and Jairo were close to the city, the demigod jetted to the third level. He blasted to the tower and landed dynamically inside the dome. No one was there. He expected to see at least one of the council members upon the crescent platform.

Jairo flew into the dome with Kairi. He would not remove the blade from her neck. "Nice place," he commented. "Is this where the aero jewel is?"

"Step inside the circle." Caim beckoned, unpleasantly. On the ground that he stood, a circle was illustrated resembling the sun. A gilded star inside the sun. Jairo stepped inside the circle never removing his hands from Kairi.

"Caim, where am I? And why is this happening?" she asked in terror. She was petite and somewhat meek. Caim was not sure what he ever saw in her. He rather not know. He believed that love is best when it is blind.

"Everything is going to be alright Kairi. I am going to get you out of here I promise," Caim told her, hoping it would put her at ease.

Caim walked to the center of the crescent platform. At the very middle below where Nehushine had sat, there was a lever. He pulled it down and something thudded underground. The ground shook for an instant. Caim stood inside the circle again. "What did you just do?" Jairo asked pressing his sword on Kairi.

"I am taking you down to the chamber of the aero

jewel," Caim answered.

Suddenly, the circle in which they stood began to descend. Soon their heads were below the floor level. The ground dropped and nothing but grey walls surrounded them.

"I almost feel sorry for toppling your city. Your architecture is similar to Ironside," Jairo said.

"You've been to the city of Ironside," Caim asked. He was surprise that his foe knew of the legendary city. A city uncharted and known by few throughout the world. "Did you topple their edifices as well?"

"I have more respect for such a sacred city. This technology reminds me of Ironside," Jairo said then stared up at the shaft way from which they came.

The floor continued to descend. Caim was stuck in a chamber with Jairo. They stared at each other down vilely. Caim then met eyes with Kairi. Jairo had released his hands from her neck. The white masked fiend threw his long black cloak over Kairi. Smoke filled his cloak and covered the girl's body. She disappeared into blackness. It was like watching someone vanish in the dark of the night. It was dark magic, shadomancy, unlike any Caim had ever seen before or read about.

"Where did you send her?" the demigod snarled.

"Do not worry. She will be fine as long as you keep your promise. I can summon her at will like a spirit from the limbo," Jairo answered and crossed his arms. "Your enemies will always use your loved ones against you. Love is a burden. A demigod should know."

"Love is the only panacea. Only love can cure the world," Caim preached. "It is people like you who hinder this world. I hope whatever you intend to do with the aero jewel is of equal worth to the damage you have done to my city."

"What I intend to do with the aero jewel is none of your business," Jairo answered.

The descending floor began to slow down. An opening on the right revealed itself as they arrived to their destination. The floor stopped with a thump. Caim walked through the opening on the right and Jairo followed behind him. They entered the chamber where the aero jewel was kept.

The chamber had diamonds and gold stones on the walls aligned throughout the perimeter. The ceiling glittered with gold shaped stars. The floor was cobbled with jade and rose quartz gemstones. It was beautiful. Anyone who entered the room was put at ease. At the very end of the chamber the aero jewel hovered heavenly on a pedestal. It was a white jewel and shined like a diamond. It was shaped like an oval and inside looked like a blue sky frozen in time. Jairo was astonished by the sight of the three female ghostly spirits that danced around the jewel naked. They orbited the jewel. The aero jewel is a remnant of Aeramus, the dragon god of air himself. The three tiny spirits sang a hymn so calming and melodic that it inspired one to join their eternal dance. Jairo paced towards the jewel. He stepped slowly gazing at the glowing aero jewel like a star of the night. It carried infinite air maju. Jairo knew of the jewel's powers. It could do unspeakable things and now that power was going to be his.

"Yes, that power will be mine. I will be able to cast every single spell that is written in the Grimoire Of The Sky," Jairo said to himself. "For so many years I have search for this. Oh, mighty Cosmus."

"You speak of Cosmus," Caim said as he allowed his foe to obtain the jewel. "Cosmus the god of space and time. You know how to enter the realm of Cosmus." Caim was suddenly intrigued by the intentions of Jairo. What could this white masked villain know of Cosmus, the realm where the Effeelions dedicated their life to find. The very reason why Caim joined the Effeelions five decades ago. Legend spoke of Cosmus, a dragon god from another realm. Unlike Aeramus who resided in Odealeous, it is said that Cosmus resided beyond the stars. Caim believed that Cosmus is the reason why he became a demigod. Had it not been for Cosmus sending him that shooting star, Caim would still be living with the monks in the Kumo Sora Mountains of the Yama country.

"I told you demigod. What I intend to do with the jewel is none of your business," Jairo said. He reached over to the aero jewel and grasped it. As soon as he touched the jewel, the hymn of the three spirits stopped and they disappeared. Jairo removed the jewel from the pedestal and he held it over his head with triumph and laughed. "Yes. I finally have it. It is mine all mine!" yelled the masked man. Then all the stones in the chamber began to lose their color. The jades and rose quartz that cobbled the floor became colorless. The diamonds and gold on the walls turned to grey stones. The chamber became dull yet Caim remained calm and still.

"You have the jewel, now give me Kairi," Caim demanded.

"Why of course. I am not one to break promises. Here, you can have the filthy human." Jairo swung his cloak, smoke billowed then opened it theatrically with a thud and Kairi flew out of the smoke.

Kairi flew across the chamber; Caim dashed forward and caught her. She had fainted. Her heart was still beating. Caim looked up at Jairo. The white masked fiend gripped the jewel and stared at it with lust.

Caim placed Kairi's body on the floor. He faced Jairo and extended an arm with an open palm. "Come to me, Aero Cosmo Jewel," Caim chanted. Jairo's right hand jerked. Jairo felt something pulling his hand as if he was arm wrestling with someone. He gripped the jewel and grunted as the unknown force tried to pull the jewel from his hand.

"No. You will not take the jewel from me, demigod," Jairo swore. He knew Caim was using his cosmic power. "I did not come all this way just to lose my treasure."

Jairo's black boots began to slide over the cobbled floor, then, he released a cloud of smoke. Caim lost his force over Jairo and when the smoke cleared, the masked man had disappeared from the chamber with the jewel.

"No! I almost had him," Caim cursed. "Not too worry. He got the jewel but he won't go very far." The demigod remained calm. He understood the power of the jewel enough to have the confidence of simply letting it go. However, if the Aero Cosmo Jewel was removed from its place, Kazenolumos was sure to fall from the sky. The very reason why the city could float in the sky for centuries was because of the jewel. The remnant of Aeramus. Caim knew he only had a few minutes to reclaim the jewel before the city began to fall. He would surely return it to its rightful place.

Caim lifted Kairi. The girl moaned but did not wake. He went back to the round floor that had taken him to the chamber. He flew up the shaft with Kairi in his arms. He ascended steadily till he reached the third level of the city in the dome of the council of seven. Once he reached the dome, Nehushine stood there with Tortori and Kazemee. Nehushine bled from his forehead. Tortori's tunic was tattered and Kazemee had blood and dust smeared over her face and tunic.

"Where are the other councils?" the demigod asked.

"We are not sure if they are still alive but that masked intruder had injured them," Kazemee answered. Her voice was shaky. Caim frowned and paced towards her.

"Please, attend to Kairi for me," Caim requested. "I know she is not allow here but I promise I will make things right again. This is all my fault."

"Caim, I cannot sense the maju of the aero jewel. Don't tell me he took it." Nehushine spoke as if he were to panic. Anyone in Kazenolumos would panic if they heard that the Aero Cosmo Jewel had been stolen. Their city would fall from the sky to the oceans of Odealeous. Nehushine clutched Caim's tunic and pulled him down two feet lower. "You are the guardian of this sanctuary; please tell me you got rid of him."

"Lord Nehushine. The intruder took the jewel but I promise I will return it," Caim said calmly.

"Without the jewel every Effeelion will be forced to flee Kazenolumos," Nehushine said and shuddered.

Caim had never seen the elder in such a nervous state. "Hurry boy. Get the remnant back or we are doomed. Our plans and goals will be ruin."

Caim placed Kairi on the floor and Kazemee cradled the girl's head. "I will take care of her," Kazemee said.

"Thank you," Caim replied and he realized that it was the first time they had actually coped with each other for the longest time.

Caim tossed his head back and looked up at the window in the ceiling of the dome. He shot through it like an arrow launched from a bow. He ascended over the city and flew a hundred feet above it. He saw that it already began to drop. Kazenolumos' base was touching the clouds below and continued to drop gradually. Caim closed his eyes and used his cosmic powers to track the Aero Cosmo Jewel. He had come in contact with it once so he knew how its maju vibrated. Every living creature in Odealeous vibrated with maju. Caim could sense life from leagues away. Air maju moved in a circular motion. With his eyes close he could feel every life force in the Yama country. He used his mind to track the maju of any creature that flew in the sky. He sensed hawks and eagles nearby. *Where could he be?* he asked the unknown as he scanned the skies below him with his mind. Cosmic energy was generated from the mind unlike maju which came from nature itself.

Caim could see everything and all the birds and creatures that flew. Still no sign of Jairo. Then Caim gazed west with cosmic energy vibrating in his head. He sensed an enormous maju moving north west of the Yama country. *That must be him*, the demigod assumed. As soon as he locked spotted it, he blasted like a meteor falling from the sky. His power pushed through the wind currents. He fell through the clouds. His body shining with purple light, the color of cosmo. In a few seconds he had flown by the Kumo Sora Montains of the Yama country. Forests and meadows streamed below him. He flew like a comet, so fast and godly that he never remembered using so much of his power. *Kairi I am sorry, I will make sure no one ever hurts you again. Effeelions hear me. I will make sure no one ever attacks our city and hurts our loved ones. Aeramus oh mighty god, heed my words. I promise to never break my vows again.*

Soon he flew over the ocean and he gazed at the horizon never losing his focus on the jewel's maju. *If only I could open a portal that would take me there*, Caim plotted but he could only open portals as far as he could see. As he jetted through the oceans north of the Yama country, he divided the waters with his speed, a godly speed. The maju of the jewel moved farther from him. He would soon catch up to its location. *Jairo can teleport with his dark magic. With black smoke he disappeared from the aero jewel's chamber. Where is he taking the jewel?* That is when Caim realized where Jairo was heading. He moved towards the islands of El Nido. Another location in Odealeous that is uncharted. Very few knew how to find the islands. Thanks to the feathered ghost team of Kazenolumos Caim had traveled the entire map. He had seen every country during his hunts for knowledge. He flew with his team of Effeelions to every corner of the world. *How does this masked man know of the islands? Perhaps he is a knowledge hunter just like the Effeelions. I still don't understand why I can't sense his maju.*

Caim pressed more power into his flight. The aero jewel was near, he gazed at the horizon and he could sense its maju just a few leagues away. *I am a demigod. No masked bastard will escape from me*, he swore.

"There he is!" Caim said once he spotted Jairo flying just miles away from him. Caim recognized Jairo's black cloak ruffling in the wind. He had the masked foe in sight. Caim used his cosmic powers and summoned a portal. The demigod flew into the oval portal and appeared flying right next to Jairo. Caim flew above Jairo. It seemed his foe had not noticed him yet. Caim dived down, throttled Jairo and they both plunged into the water.

Caim could survive underwater for days however, Jairo was still human. Or so the demigod thought. Caim continued to throttle the masked man. Jairo had no air to breath and he still held the aero jewel in his right hand. The jewel glowed underwater and its light scared away nearby fishes. *Give me the jewel and I will let you live*, Caim communicated with Jairo mentally. Jairo heard the words in his mind and replied with a laugh. A hysterical laugh as if he were mocking the demigod. Then ink began to cover Jairo. He was being swallowed by darkness much like his black smoke. Caim refused to let him go and got caught in the ink underwater. They both disappeared and then reappeared up high in the sky.

Jairo panted and his black clothes were soaked. The masked man would not let go of the aero jewel.

"You think you won," Jairo said. He coughed then snickered. "I will let you have this victory. Go ahead take the jewel." Jairo's arms were weak. His arms hanged from the sides of his shoulder.

Caim snatched the jewel. His hands were soaked as well as his tunic. His pure white hair was damped. Using his left hand Caim gripped Jairo's neck and gagged his foe.

"After what you have done, you don't deserve to be

kept alive," Caim said. "However, I will spare you, but, I will keep my eye on you." Caim released Jairo's neck. The masked man hovered before the demigod. Caim used his cosmic power to control his foe. He then placed his hand over Jairo's forehead and sent a shock into Jairo's mind. The masked man felt as though someone had wacked him on the head. Caim let him go and the masked man hovered unsteadily in the air.

"What did you do to me?" Jairo asked in terror.

"You were using dark magic to hide your maju. Very clever, however, I removed the spell you had on yourself. From now on I will be able to sense your maju no matter where you are in Odealeous. I leave you here in middle of the ocean. I will allow you to live but you must find your own way. Goodbye." With those last words Caim blasted through the sky back to Kazenolumos to save the city from falling.

"You have not seen the last of me demigod!" Jairo yelled as he watched the demigod fly away with his treasure.

Part 3

Caim flew with Kairi in his arms. He was taking her back to Yumemaru town. This would be the last time he would see her. She had awakened hours ago after Caim retrieved the Aero Cosmo Jewel.   She rested her head on his chest and gazed at her lover. He was focus on returning her home and had not spoken for an hour. His snow white hair swayed with the wind and carried a serious look on his face. He seemed sad and heartbroken and she knew why. Caim had explained everything. He told her about his cosmic powers and how he was a demigod, guardian of Kazenolumos. He apologized for all the lies he had told her to prevent her from discovering his true self. He explained to her how he broke his vows to the Effeelions to be with her.

Caim wished he could shed tears but demigods don't cry. Caim had not cried in five decades. His godly body did not feel sadness or depression. Kairi had trouble believing him at first but the evidence was right before her. She was in his arms chiliads of feet in the air and saw how he manipulated the wind just by swaying his hand. Kairi had met Nehushine and the Effeelions. She felt Caim's pain. His duty was to the Effeelions and vowed to never wed or have children with a mortal woman. He was sure Kairi was pregnant with his half breed child.

He had broken his vow twice.

Caim still struggled to decide. *Perhaps being a human is not so bad*, he said to himself. His fleshy desires still ran through him like warm bugs with a sliver of ecstasy. However, he could not take his eyes off his commitment. His goal was to discover the realm of Cosmus with the Effeelions. He wanted to know the unknown and see sights that mortal souls only dreamt of. He struggled to decide like a child with too many options. His head spun just by thinking about it.

"In about eight months I will give birth to your son," Kairi whispered in Caim's ears. The wind was warm and soothing. Caim flew slowly to the Yama country to savor the moment he still had with her. He looked at her and kissed her.

"How do you know?" he asked.

"A woman knows," she said. "I just want you to know that you can always come and visit your son whenever you want my love." Their eyes meet and Caim smiled. He loved her narrow eyes and her accent of the Yama country. He wished he could shed tears and cry. He wanted to feel that humanly pain of lost that he once felt five decades ago before he became a demigod. *Maybe being a human is not so bad*, he said to himself again. *Am I willing to simply give up Kairi for the life I have with the Effeelions?*

"I will miss you and I will tell your son all about his father," Kairi said as she caressed his cheek and his hair. "I will always love you. Demigod or no demigod."

"I will find a way I promise. My dear," Caim said gently. After a few minutes of flying, Caim left Kairi in Yumemaru town. He lay with her one last time before he departed and promised to return to see the birth of his child. He would count the days and keep her in his heart. He was going to be a father soon and that filled his heart with joy.

Caim flew back to Kazenolumos and helped clean the debris. The Effeelions worked hard to rebuild the first and second level of the city. The ivory stones were difficult to reconnect and it took twenty Effeelions to lift a stone column. Only fifty Effeelions were found dead and the people made a ritual to mourn those who had fallen and made sure they found their way to the realm of light.

It took five days and nights to restore everything to the way it was before Jairo attacked. After the restoration Caim and Nehushine went to the chamber of the Aero Cosmo Jewel. It was back on its pedestal and the three nude female spirits sang their eternal hymn and danced around the jewel once more. They stood by it and watched it glow as its light reflected off the diamonds, gold and other gemstones that cobbled the chamber.

"We must relocate Kazenolumos. This is our only home. We must make sure that such catastrophe does not happen again," Nehushine lectured. "I will use the power of the Aero Cosmo Jewel and place our sanctuary in a different area of the Yama country."

"So you will move the city away from the Kumo Sora Mountains," Caim said.

"I have not decided where but the city must be positioned in a more peaceful area. Perhaps to the east," Nehushine replied, stroking his long pointy goateed bear. "I must speak with the council about this."

"Lord Nehushine, why have you brought me to the chamber?" Caim asked.

"Ah, yes, my good boy." Nehushine chuckled. "I brought you here to tell you about an unusual maju coming from the Aero Cosmo Jewel. You see, ever since you retrieved the jewel from that white masked intruder, I have been sensing some soothing maju from the jewel. I can't explain what it is exactly but it seemed to have reacted to your emotions, Caim."

Caim scratched his head for a moment. Nehushine spoke but Caim thought the old Effeelion had not finished his sentence. "Well, continue on old man. How are my emotions causing the jewel to react?"

"That is what I am trying to understand. It is not something you can find in a tome or ancient scroll but rather something from the heart. The 'soul,' for lack of a better word. I found wisps of your maju in the jewel and I believe you have nothing to do with that but rather the jewel chose your maju for reasons I have yet to comprehend. At first I thought that the jewel reacted well to intellect since that is what the element of air represents. The element of air represents freedom, intelligence, creativity, spirituality and knowledge. That is only some of its virtues however, I feel as though something is eluding me. Like a missing piece of the puzzle or a part of a recipe that I forgot to add." Then Nehushine shifted his body towards Caim with arms crossed. "Tell me, what was running through you at that time when you chased Jairo to retrieve the jewel?"

"I felt as though I was going to lose everything I love," Caim answered and frowned. "I felt great guilt. It was my fault that Jairo had discovered Kazenolumos. I lead him here. Not only that but I put Kairi in danger. I swore that none of this will happen again. I used a large amount of power and I was able to find Jairo flying over the northern seas of the Yama country. I wanted to kill him for almost destroying everything I love."

"That must be it then!" Nehushine jumped. "Love. That is the key. I believe that is what the jewel has been reacting to."

"How can you be so sure, Lord Nehushine," Caim questioned. "Perhaps the Sapphire Cosmo Jewel would feed off human emotions but I am sure the aero jewel is different."

Nehushine stared back at the aero jewel. "Some things are not easily explained by simply doing research or reading books my boy. The human soul is a complex thing," Nehushine lectured. "When people are in a trance, unspeakable things can happen." Nehushine fell silent as he continued to gaze at the jewel.

"Let's say that the jewel has chosen me for whatever reason. What would it mean for me?" Caim asked and contemplated everything that had happened when Jairo attacked.

"I am not sure," Nehushine replied. "However, my instinct tells me that this can lead us to a new discovery." Then the old Effeelion looked at Caim with a wide smile. "My good demigod I want you to continue to visit that human girl."

Caim jerked his head to Nehushine. The old Effeelion was encouraging him to break his vow. "Umm...Lord Nehushine is your head spinning or perhaps you had too much to drink?" Caim asked sarcastically, still in disbelief of the old man's suggestion.

"You heard me clearly. I want you to continue visiting that human girl," Nehushine repeated. "Something good has hatched out of an egg we have been afraid of for such a long time." The old Effeelion continued. "Love seems to be one of the keys into entering the realm of Cosmus. Somehow your humanly desires triggered an unknown power in the aero jewel. Forget about the vows you made. I, Nehushine, the leader of the council of seven and the Effeelions allow you to pursue your humanly happiness. I now realize that for the last five decades we have been depriving you of something very powerful. I am sorry my good friend. Trying to appease to your humanly desires won't prevent us from finding a way into the realm of Cosmus. You have taught me a valuable lesson."

When Nehushine finished his speech, Caim was somewhat confuse. Although he did understand that love had somehow triggered the aero jewel's powers, he wondered what it had to do with discovering the realm of Cosmus.

Cosmus was pure cosmic power. The power of the stars and infinity. Cosmus meant no limitations. According to what the Effeelions had taught Caim, the realm of Cosmus is where everything started. The genesis of all life began with Cosmus. Caim concluded that only by finding power sources similar to his the Effeelions would be able to enter the realm of Cosmus. *Therefore how can the emotion of love be one of the keys to finding the realm*, Caim mulled with a bit of frustration.

Nehushine walked out of the chamber and to the round elevator that took them to the council's dome. "Wait!" Caim called. He joined Nehushine in the elevator. "You will explain this to me diplomatically, Lord Nehushine," Caim demanded.

"Sorry my boy, but this time I don't have the correct words to explain my theory. Nor is this a hypothesis that we can test out in the lab or library. I ask that you have faith in my theory." Nehushine told Caim and once the elevator reached the council's dome, the old Effeelion flew out of the window and to the lower levels of the city. Caim was left perplexed by Nehushine's theory. *Love is one of the keys to finding the realm of Cosmus.* It kept bouncing and ricocheting inside Caim's head.

Later that night Caim refused to stop thinking about what Nehushine had told him. He thought about swooping down from Kazenolumos and visit Kairi again since the old man had changed the rules. Caim was now allowed to see her whenever he wanted. He did not have to worry about breaking vows or making the council worry. However, he decided to go to the library in the first level of Kazenolumos.

Caim flew from his floating island. The two moons
and stars were above him and he felt his powers
simmering. He grew with the stars and mystery of the
night. His mind worked better during the night. As he
flew towards the sky city, Caim saw many Effeelions
jetting out of the first level. He heard their shrieks
and yells for help. From afar he spotted no
destruction like when Jairo had attacked yet he blasted
towards the city pressing more of his power into his
flight. His heart pounded at his chest. *Please don't tell
me is that masked man in black*, he prayed to Aeramus.
With an incredible speed he arrived at the first level of
Kazenolumos.

Effeelions ran away and flew out of the city like a
swarm of geese. No taller than four feet, they seemed
like scared children to him for a moment. Then he
gazed at the scene from where they ran. In the middle
of the grey marble stone streets, Caim saw the masked
man again. *How did I not sense his arrival*, the demigod
stopped to think. Caim dashed over the marble
streets, his feet gliding over the floor. The masked
man Jairo was being surrounded by hundreds of
Effeelions. The brave Effeelions that tried to defend
their sanctuary had their air spells ready with open
palms. Jairo stood there as if he refused to defend
himself. His long black cloak cascaded off his
shoulders. He leered Caim with one eye as he arrived
to the scene.

"All Effeelions evacuate this area and allow me to handle this fiend," Caim commanded. They did not hesitate. They huddled out of the street area.

"I am not here to cause destruction," Jairo said. His voice echoed from the "X" opening of his mask.

"That was my first guess. I hope you learned from the punishment I gave you last time you came," Caim said.

"I would not call that punishment," Jairo replied with no sign of hostility. "You are too soft to be called a demigod. You are a child in a man's body. You are not worthy of those cosmic powers you wield. I have come here today for your demise. I will strip you of your 'god like powers.'"

Caim crossed his arms confidently and raised his chin. His posture was mighty and he elevated a few inches off the marble floor. "A challenge is it…then I accept. This time I will make sure your soul drops to Necrovania. You are too dangerous to be kept alive. I sense darkness in you."

"I will prove to you that you are no god. You could not even sense my presence till you saw your pointy ear friends running away," Jairo said. "At first I wanted the Aero Cosmo Jewel but your cosmic powers are far more valuable."

"If you want to battle then let's move this out of the

sanctuary," Caim said.

Suddenly a portal opened behind Jairo just like last time. An oval mirror hovering behind the masked fiend. Jairo was being sucked into the portal. Caim dashed and kicked the masked man in. The demigod then jumped inside the portal and he was now in the open sky above the clouds far from Kazenolumos.

The portal closed behind the demigod. Jairo fell down to the clouds. As Caim waited for his foe to recover from the fall, he raised his cosmic power. It was a full moon and the stars shined brighter. He was at his fullest. *There will be no dawn for you Jairo, you will die,* the demigod swore.

Abruptly, Jairo blasted out of the clouds and streamed towards Caim. The demigod slashed the air and with a wisp of his maju he created beams of razor wind that could cut through flesh. The razor wind sliced Jairo in half. Caim smiled but quickly saw through the illusion. The cleaved body of Jairo shattered into crying crows. The black birds swarmed towards Caim. Their eyes were an angry red that glowed in the night. The demigod snapped his fingers and from the unknown, spheres of light appeared by the dozens. The glowing spheres swelled and with a buzzing sound they drifted towards the crows in a circular motion. When the crows came in contact with the spheres they detonated like fireworks of a carnival. A horrible death for crows but a beautiful sight for

Caim.

Smoke rose from the explosion and Jairo appeared hovering in the sky as the smoke cleared. His cloak had been tattered up to his girth.

"I told you I will show no mercy. You have walked into your own doom," Caim said hoarsely. He did not remember becoming so violent. For so long Caim had been taught that killing is wrong. When he was a monk his elders taught him that killing is bad karma. Even the Effeelions told him never to kill. Use killing as an absolute last resort. *I will slay all evil*, Caim thought as the words from his teachers ran through his head. For some reason he still could not sense Jairo's maju. However, the masked man reeked of darkness. Caim knew that his foe's intentions were of the underworld. *I thought I dispelled his dark magic to be able to sense his maju.*

"You will not triumph today. Demigod," Jairo rasped. From within his cloak he drew a black sword. The sword was made of rare steel that Caim detested.

"Your kaminyte sword won't be enough," Caim yelled and opened a portal behind Jairo. The masked man was sucked into the portal and reappeared in front of Caim. The demigod delivered a stinging kick to the head and Jairo was sent flying with pain pulsing on the side of his head. It was a direct hit and Jairo's head spun and quickly began to ache. Using his maju he stopped his body from falling again. He had never experienced such a devastating blow. Caim's kick felt like running into a bull. Jairo's head stung and he thought that his cranium had been fractured. *No I won't lose today*, the masked man thought. *Your power will be mine.*

Black smoke rose from Jairo's cloak and from within the shadows, he pulled a bizarre shape tool. It looked like a sea shell with jewels of all colors bedecked on it. Inside the shell was an orb that glowed with an amethyst color. Jairo gripped the curved hilt of the shell. There was another piece of jewel that glowed white above the orb and curved over the shell like a swan's neck. It was a beautiful master piece that seemed to be crafted by heavenly hands yet it was being held by the claws of a fiend. Jairo held it up extending his arm. The orb inside of the shell glowed as if it was reacting to something.

"What in Odealeous is that?" the demigod whispered. His eyes widened with awe. He gazed at the object Jairo held, mesmerized until he remembered what it was. "No!" Caim shouted. "It can't be. How did you? No-no-no there is absolutely no way you could have found it. I got rid of it and made sure that no one would ever find it."

"Yes. Fear the very tool you used to become immortal," Jairo said and chuckled. The cold wind of the night rushed through him. Through the opening in his mask for the left eye he stared at the object. "The cosmo lantern. So powerful, so rare and beautiful. I wonder how a kid such as you was able to get your hands on it. I scavenged through Necrovania and trekked through Odealeous to find this magnificent tool. I found it hidden in the deepest caves and tunnels of the West Mountains in the Yama country. According to the dragon bible there are only a dozen of these cosmo lanterns. It is said that the first mages in the Garden of Eden crafted these. The dragon bible says that during the very first civilization, people had a deeper connection to the god we know as Cosmus. It also says that some mages were able to enter the realm of Cosmus but no historical trace has been found."

Caim panicked by simply staring at the cosmo lantern. The very tool that he used to become a demigod. The tool he used to absorb a shooting star. Back then even as a young man, Caim's instinct told him of a higher being that existed beyond the stars. That shooting star was but a tiny fragment of the power of Cosmus. Caim then swallowed the energy that the cosmo lantern had absorbed and cosmic power began to flow through him. He remembered feeling the powers of the stars that night. Caim used that power to stop the war between the United Pathways country and the Yama country. Now he was afraid of losing that power. Jairo was going to use the cosmo lantern and drain Caim of his powers. *No, I won't allow it,*

Caim told himself but he began to feel his powers being drained. The cosmo lantern homed for the energy it lost and tugged Caim's powers. *I can feel my energy slipping away. No, I am a demigod. I won't lose to this masked bastard. If I lose my powers I won't be able to help the Effeelions anymore.*

Jairo raised the cosmo lantern over his head. The orb illuminated the night and painted the clouds below with an amethyst color. A purple color. The color of cosmic energy. Caim began to sweat. He opened a portal and reached inside the oval window. Caim's hand appeared behind Jairo as the masked man held the cosmo lantern. Caim gripped Jairo's cloak and pulled him with great force out of the portal window. Jairo then twisted his body and swung his cosmo lantern across Caim's head. Normally Caim would not feel much physical pain. However, this blow contained his own cosmic energy. It felt like being wacked with a brick. His head spun as he fell from the sky and for the first time in decades he got a headache. His forehead was bleeding, his power continued to slip away and his snow white hair gradually changed to grey.

Using his cosmic power, Caim was able to ease his fall. *I am going to have to use everything I have,* Caim thought. *Either Jairo dies or I lose my powers.* The demigod blasted up towards the moon. Wind whistling all around and he converted it to razor

wind. He summoned a powerful gust towards Jairo.
The masked man was an air magus as well. He
deflected the winds and shot bullets of air at Caim.
The wind followed no current in their battle. The
wind gusted in all directions as the two air mages
fought.

Caim jetted through the sky directly towards Jairo and
tackled the masked man like a ram running through a
wall. They both fell through the clouds. Caim had his
arms wrapped around Jairo's girth. The masked man
had no choice but to fall. He almost lost grip of the
cosmo lantern. Caim tried to snatch the lantern from
Jairo but he felt his body weakening.

Jairo hammered Caim on the head with the lantern
again. Pain exploded and the demigod screamed and
lost grip of Jairo. They drifted away from each other
in the sky. Caim had pushed them down towards the
oceans of the Yama country.

"You are no demigod. You are still a boy," Jairo
yelled and laughed. "How dare you call yourself a
god? You are not worthy of this power."

"Who are you to judge?" Caim snarled with his hand
on his bleeding forehead. He had not bled in decades.
He had not felt such pain in so long; it did not exist
for him until now. "I was chosen. Blessed by
Aeramus, the air dragon god himself. And you-you
are just a fiend trying to take what is not yours by

force. A power hungry bastard who bullies his way through to get what he wants. I cannot allow someone like you to possess this power and bring chaos upon Odealeous."

Caim extended his hands. Purple steam rose from his body. Cosmic energy evaporated. He opened a portal right in front of himself. This time a larger portal. An oval two hundred feet wide. Inside the portal it was pitch black like the mouth of a behemoth. "Look into your death Jairo!" Caim yelled. The portal was a window to the stars. Inside portal Jairo could see the stars up close like looking into a telescope. Something was approaching as he stared. It looked like a boulder on fire.

"This is a portal into the realm beyond the sky," Jairo said with excitement. "Impressive. That power will be mine."

Suddenly something flew out of the portal. It was an enormous rock set on fire, the size of a titans head. Jairo's body became paralyzed by the cosmic energy of the rock.

"It looks like you have never seen a comet before. Its energy paralyzes any life force that stands in its way," Caim said with a long smirk. "Rest in the darkest pits of Necrovania, Jairo. May the dragon god of darkness feasts upon your soul."

Jairo could not move. He was stuck in mid air staring at the comet as it fell on him, soon to drive him deep into the ocean. The comet was close now and casted a colossal shadow. Jairo snickered. Although he could not move he still remained calm. His arm was already raised up holding the cosmo lantern. He knew that the lantern was absorbing the energy of the comet. Once the comet reached him, it shattered into rocks, boulders, pebbles and ores. It turned into a rain of stones. Jairo was then able to move again.

"You see. You don't know how to use your powers," Jairo told the demigod. "You are still a boy in puberty. Still green and learning from his masters. That power deserves a more discipline user. Once I strip you of your powers you won't have much to worry about. After all, you wanted to be human again."

Caim did not answer to Jairo's remark. A gust of wind blew and billowed Caim's white hair and filled his sleeves with air. As the gust blew, the demigod disappeared right before Jairo's eyes.

"The blind wind dance," Jairo said. "I know that spell. You do not frighten me, demigod. I specialize in air magic. Your spell won't …."

Before he could end his sentence, Jairo received a blow to his solar plexus. All the air in his lungs left him and the masked man almost lost grip of the cosmo lantern. Jairo continued to take blows to his body. He could not see Caim but the demigod delivered blows to the head and to the torso. Caim's spell made him invisible. Jairo could not see Caim unless he was using the same spell. Finally, Caim throttled Jairo while invisible. Caim's hands were like a hawk's talons around Jairo neck. The masked man could not breathe or speak. The demigod then became visible again.

"I rarely use the *blind wind dance* spell," Caim said. "Thank you for pushing me this far but this fight is over."

"I...don't...think...so...gack!" Jairo struggled to speak. From inside the blackness of his cloak he drew his black sword again and drove it through Caim's belly. The demigod groaned and let go of Jairo. The masked man coughed heavily.

"You can't get rid of me that easily. Stupid boy," Jairo insulted and drove his black sword deeper into Caim. The demigod coughed blood on Jairo's shoulder. The kaminyte steel gave him a fever and it weakened his body. Caim's body began to shiver like winter cold but he refused to be weak. He throttled Jairo again and plunged the blade farther through his body.

"If I am to die then you are coming with me. To Necrovania or the realm of light. Either way I cannot allow you to live," Caim whispered. He wrapped his arms around Jairo and crushed the masked man as if he was trying to squeeze the blood out of his foe. With a fragment of his cosmic power he opened a portal and Caim flew through it while crushing Jairo.

They reappeared in the south west shores of the Yama country. They landed with a thump so loud it scared seagulls away. They rolled over the sand away from each other. Jairo's mask had been fractured. Caim's hair became a dark grey color, gradually turning black. The demigod found the bit of strength he had left and stood up. He ran over to Jairo while the masked man was still down. Caim removed the mask and saw the face of a young man with blood smeared over his mouth. *So young and such malice,* were Caim's only thoughts. He placed his hand on Jairo's forehead and it glowed a purple light.

"I will now remove your ability to cast magic. Your connection with the mystic arts will be canceled." Caim pressed his hand on Jairo's forehead. Jairo immediately felt his mind numbing. Caim closed the doors inside Jairo's mind and sealed the pathways of his soul that connected to the elements. It took an enormous amount of his own cosmic power to remove Jairo's magical abilities.

"No!" Jairo yelled. "My magic! No! Not My magic!"

Jairo's mind felt numb and his body weak as if he had lost weight. He could not feel the maju of the wind.

He could no longer sense the magical power of nature anymore. "I am going to have to start over again," he said as he stood up, legs wobbling.

The cosmo lantern lay on the sands of the shore being washed by the ocean waves and foam. Caim looked at it and saw the orb glowing, still absorbing his power. He paced towards the shore. His feet dug into the sand and the water was up to his ankles soaking his shoes. He looked at his reflection in the water and saw that his hair was now black. From white to black. He was no longer a demigod. The cosmo lantern had drained all his powers. He was purely human again. He no longer felt that elevating energy of the stars. His eyes felt warm and his heart heavy and for the first time in five decades he shed a tear. *I miss this feeling*, he said to himself. *I can feel again. I am no longer a solid soul. I can die. I am mortal.* Caim cried but a deep part of him was happy. *I guess one cannot have everything*, he thought. *No, I will have everything. There is plenty of time.* Caim took one last look at his reflection in the water. He smiled at his reflection and turned back to Jairo.

Jairo dragged his body over the sand trying to reach the cosmo lantern. Caim ran and stomped on Jairo's hand. He lifted the cosmo lantern and gazed at the energy pulsing inside the orb.

"I will be taking this. I will make sure the cosmo lantern will never be in the hands of malice again,"

Caim said. "You are no longer a threat. You can crawl back to where ever you came from or you can start a new life and forget your evil ways."

Jairo snickered as he stood up. His joints were weak and it seemed as though he lost weight. His black garments wrinkled over his body. His clothes were no longer tight on his skin.

"What are you going to do now? You are willing to give up your god like powers for a mortal life?" Jairo asked and cackled. "You are so weak. If you allow me to live I swear I will come back and haunt you. I will find you again and take the cosmo lantern from you. Then one day I will be a god and I will destroy Kazenolumos and take their collection of knowledge."

"As I said. You are no longer a threat. You will have to start from the beginning," Caim said. "The only way your air magic will return is by retraining yourself. As for me, I have decided that I won't return to Kazenolumos. I will live a mortal life and I will hide this cosmo lantern until the day that I must use it again. Farewell." With those last words Caim left Jairo in the south west shores of the Yama country. Caim trekked to Yumemaru town where his beloved lived.

Months after he defeated Jairo and walked as a human again, a group of Effeelions found Caim. It was the Feathered Ghost team that Caim would travel the world with. His friend Lanalynn with dozens of other Effeelions found him in Yumemaru town. Caim said he did not want to return to Kazenolumos. He explained to them how he lost his power. The Effeelions thanked him for all the years he had protected them. Caim still wanted to stay connected to the Effeelions. They always welcomed him with open arms. He told the Effeelions that he wanted to live as a human for a few years before he went back to living as a god.

"There is something beautiful about being human that I was unable to grasp as a demigod. Being a demigod was a great experience. However, I believe that there are answers to be found by living a mortal life. I believe that to find the realm of Cosmus I must first know why the dragon gods created us."

Thank you for reading.

I am not the best at writing romance but with Fall Of A Demigod I thought I give it a try. I said that if I ever write romance there would have to be lots of magic and action as well. This was a fun story to write. There is a lot of me in Caim, from my teen years. To be human or not to be…that is the question.

If you like this story I want you to know that Caim will be making appearances in my other books. I recommend signing up to the mailing list for release dates.

http://ajmartinezauthor.com/mailing-list/

If you like this book please post a REVIEW where ever you bought it from, Amazon, Barnes and Nobles, iBooks, Kobo, Smashwords. Share with your friends.

Let's stay connected.

http://ajmartinezauthor.com/

https://twitter.com/ajmartinezautho

https://www.facebook.com/fantasyauthorajmartinez

Novels and short stories by A.J. Martinez

Scarlet Quest

The Ungifted Elf

Rift Of Chaos (coming late 2015)

A.J Martinez

Made in the USA
Charleston, SC
24 June 2015